Stockyards

Stockyards

Rod Bellville and Cheryl Walsh Bellville

Carolrhoda Books, Inc., Minneapolis

The authors would like to thank Curt Zimmerman of the Livestock Market Institute in South St. Paul, Minnesota, the John Barber Auction Company, and all of the people pictured in this book for their help in the making of *Stockyards*.

LIBRARY OF CONGRESS CATALOG IN PUBLICATION DATA

Bellville, Rod.
  Stockyards.

  Summary: Describes the activities that take place at
a large stockyard including the jobs done by yardmen,
brokers, packer buyers, dealer buyers, auctioneers, and
others. Also describes how the animals are transported
from ranches to stockyards and a typical auction.
  1. Cattle trade—United States—Juvenile literature.
2. Stockyards—United States—Juvenile literature.
[1. Cattle trade. 2. Stockyards] I. Bellville, Cheryl
Walsh II. Title
HD9433.U4B44 1984   636.08'31   83-18839
ISBN 0-87614-224-2

1 2 3 4 5 6 7 8 9 10 93 92 91 90 89 88 87 86 85 84

for Luke, our young stockman

6   How would a busy rancher sell you one hamburger?

What would a butcher do with a trainload of cattle?

Imagine a rancher driving a herd of cattle down a city street, stopping at every butcher shop along the way to sell a steer or two. Think of the confusion if 50 other ranchers were to do the same thing. This is why stockyards exist: to solve the rancher's problem of how to sell large numbers of animals and the butcher's problem of how to buy small quantities of meat.

The food we eat comes to us from all over the country. For example, fruit often comes from the southern states because the climate there is warm enough for fruit to grow year round. Much of the meat we eat comes to us from states like Wyoming or Wisconsin where the climate may be too dry or the land too hilly to grow crops but where cattle or sheep can be raised. The animals graze on the grass or are fed grain which their bodies turn into meat or milk.

When the time comes for animals to be sold, they are usually transported to a stockyard. The link between the farm or the ranch and the stockyard is the trucker.

A trucker's day starts early in the morning and is spent picking up animals ready to go to market. A trucker may haul animals belonging to more than one farmer on the same trip. Careful records must be kept so that each farmer will be paid for all of his or her livestock. 11

After arriving at the stockyard, the trucker checks in all of the animals with a *yardman*.

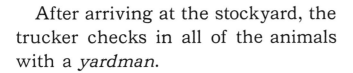

The yardman sends the animals to a *selling agency* (also called a *commission* agency) where they are sorted into pens according to size, breed, sex, age and weight, and quality. The selling agency will be responsible for selling the animals.

There are 10 selling agencies at this stockyard. Eight of them are private businesses, but 2 are owned by groups of farmers. These are called *cooperatives*.

When the animals reach their pens they are given plenty of food and fresh water. Cattle and sheep are fed hay. Each agency keeps from 1 to 5 truckloads on hand. A truck can carry about 600 bales, each weighing from 40 to 90 pounds.

Hogs are fed corn. The 6 agencies in the hog barn each have a bin holding 400 to 500 bushels. Young hogs, called *feeder pigs,* are fed fresh rolled oats. Each agency uses 8 to 9 bushels a week.

The people who sell animals are called *market men* or *commission men* because they receive a commission, or payment, for each animal they sell, and because they are usually men. They show the animals to all interested buyers and sell them to the one who offers to pay the highest price.

Most animals are sold on the same day they arrive at the stockyard, but if the farmer and the market man think they can get a better price on the next day, the stock may be held over for a day or so. Prices can go up or down daily due to consumer demand, holidays, the number of animals available at the stockyard, or the amount of meat that meat-packers have on hand.

Some buyers are looking for *finished* animals ready to be slaughtered (killed). Others are looking for young or thin stock that will go to a feedlot to be finished. Some buyers want male animals because they grow faster and produce more meat. Others want females because they are less expensive or because they will be used for breeding (producing offspring).

There are three types of buyers at a stockyard. *Packer buyers* buy slaughter animals for meat-packing plants. *Order buyers* buy animals for customers who have ordered a specific size, type, and number of animals from them. *Dealer buyers* buy animals that they think they can resell for a higher price.

When one buyer at a time looks at and agrees to buy animals, it is called a *private treaty sale*.

19

When many buyers look at the animals at the same time, it is called
an *auction*.

At an auction the animals are still sorted according to size, breed, age and weight, sex, and quality, but the animals come to the buyers instead of the buyers walking around from pen to pen. The buyers can sit and watch as different groups, called *lots*, of animals go through the sale ring.

The floor of this auction ring is a scale. It weighs all the animals on it at once. A sign shows the buyers the average weight of each animal on the scale and what the animals cost per pound.

The person who sells the livestock at an auction is called the *auctioneer*. The buyers make *bids* (offer a price) on the lot of animals up for sale. The auctioneer repeats the highest bid and asks for a higher one so rapidly that it is sometimes hard to understand what's being said unless you have spent a lot of time at auctions. Auctioneers are employed by the stockyard. They auction off the animals of all the selling agencies.

This is a feeder pig auction. Feeder pigs are about 8 weeks old and weigh about 40 pounds. Whoever buys them will feed them for about 4 months until they weigh 200 pounds. Then the pigs will come back to the stockyard to be sold as slaughter hogs.

24

Several lots of pigs can go through this ring at once. It is divided by swinging gates so that no one has to wait while the pigs come and go. Pigs are not weighed in this ring. The market man estimates (guesses) their weight and tells the auctioneer the price at which the bidding should start. Livestock buyers are also very good at estimating weights. They have to be in order to know what they are paying per pound for the animals they are buying.

A third way of selling animals is called the *Australian method*. This is a moving auction. The auctioneer walks from pen to pen and the bidders walk with him. This photograph shows a calf auction being conducted in the Australian method.

Except for feeder pigs, every animal that goes through the stockyard is carefully weighed by the stockyard's *weighmaster* after it has been sold.

These young dairy *heifers* (young females) will go to a farm where they will grow up to become milk cows.

Livestock returning to the country for breeding or milking must be tested for disease by the stockyard veterinarian. A blood sample is taken from every cow or bull over six months old or weighing about 400 pounds or more and checked for diseases such as brucellosis (broo-suh-LOW-sus) and tuberculosis. Diseased animals are not allowed to return to the country. They are traced to the farm from which they came so that the other animals on that farm can be tested as well. This prevents sick animals from spreading their illnesses to healthy animals and to people. Animals under six months old rarely have these diseases, so they don't have to be tested.

When the animals have been sold, the purpose of the stockyard has been accomplished. From here the animals will go on to whatever destinations their buyers have in mind; some to feedlots to grow bigger, some to meat-packing plants to be made into food, and some to farms to become milk cows or breeding animals which will produce more pigs, lambs, or calves to be sold at the stockyard.

Glossary

auction: a sale of livestock attended by a number of possible buyers. The animals are sold to the person who offers to pay the highest price.

Australian method: a moving auction. The auctioneer walks from pen to pen, and the bidders go with him.

bid: an offer of a price

breed: a classification of animal; for example, a milk cow might be a Jersey, a Holstein, a Guernsey, or any of a number of other breeds. When used as a verb, to breed means to produce offspring.

breeding animals: animals that are raised to produce offspring

commission man: a man who sells animals at a stockyard and receives a payment, called a commission, for each animal he sells. The commission man represents the farmer or rancher at the stockyard.

cooperative: an organization owned by the people using its services, in this case, a selling agency owned by farmers and ranchers

dealer buyers: people who buy animals that they plan to resell at a higher price

farmer: a person who raises crops and/or livestock

feeder pigs: young hogs (about 8 weeks old) weighing about 40 pounds

feedlot: a place where animals are finished before they are slaughtered

finished: fed and raised to the best condition and quality for meat

heifer: a young cow, especially one that has not yet had a calf

lot: group

market man: see commission man

meat-packing plant: a place where livestock is slaughtered and packed as meat; also simply called a packing plant

order buyers: people who take orders for animals in advance, then buy animals at a stockyard to fill those orders

packer buyers: people who buy animals for meat-packing plants

private treaty sale: a sale at which one buyer at a time looks at and agrees to buy animals, as opposed to an auction where many buyers bid on the animals at once

rancher: a person who owns or operates a ranch for the production of livestock

slaughter: kill, especially the killing of livestock

weighmaster: a person at a stockyard who weighs each animal after it has been sold

yardman: a person at a stockyard who checks in the animals and delivers them to a selling agency